What Lily Goose

by Annabelle Sumera

illustrated by Lorinda Bryan Cauley

 GOLDEN PRESS
Western Publishing Company, Inc.
Racine, Wisconsin

Fourth Printing, 1980

Lily Goose was taking a walk. She looked this way and that way. She was searching for something special for her friends.

Then she saw something round and yellow on the ground.

"What a big seed I have found!" she said. "I will take this seed to Big Tom Turkey. He will plant this seed, and something good will grow — something good for all of us."

Big Tom Turkey strutted over to take a look. "No, no," he said. "That will not grow, Lily Goose."

He strutted back to the barnyard.

"Well," said Lily Goose, "then, I will look some more."

Soon she came to the water. There she saw something long and orange. "Now I have found something good," she said.

Three ducks came toward the water. "Come here," called Lily Goose. "Here is a long orange worm for your dinner. Come and catch this long orange worm."

The three ducks looked at the long orange thing. "Quack, quack, quack," they said, shaking their heads. "That is not a worm, Lily Goose, and besides, we do not eat worms."

The three ducks paddled into the water and swam off in a line. Then they ducked their heads and turned tail-up in the water.

"Well," said Lily Goose, "then, I will look some more."

Soon she came to something in the grass. It was hard and cold and shiny.

"Now I have found something pretty and useful. Maybe Black Cow will like this," said Lily Goose.

The black and white cow was munching grass nearby. She raised her head
and asked, "What is pretty and useful,
Lily Goose?"

"This shiny thing is pretty to look at,"
said Lily Goose, "and it will keep you
cool on hot days."

The black and white cow raised her
eyes to the sky. "No, Lily Goose," she
said. "It is pretty and useful now, but
it will not last long."

Black Cow switched her tail and went
back to munching grass.

"Well," said Lily Goose, "then, I will look some more."

She came to a big rock. Next to it she saw something yellow.

"Oh," she said, "now I have found something for Smiley Pig. It is a yellow apple. He likes apples."

Smiley Pig was resting in the shade
on the other side of the big rock. He got
up to see what Lily Goose had found.
"Where is the apple?" he asked.

"Here," said Lily Goose. "It is round like an apple, and it is smooth like an apple. It must be a yellow apple."

Smiley Pig sniffed it. "No, Lily Goose, it is not an apple," he said.

Smiley Pig went back to rest in the shade beside the big rock.

Lily Goose walked a little more. She came to the end of the path. She saw something big and long and green.

"Oh, oh!" she said. "This is something Smiley Pig likes. This is a big green watermelon."

Lily Goose gave the big green thing a poke. It went *pop!*

Lily Goose fell back in surprise. "My, oh, my!" she said. "I guess it was not a watermelon."

Lily Goose walked away slowly. Her head hung down. She was not happy.

"My seed would not grow," she said. "My orange worm was not right for the ducks. My shiny thing would not last. Smiley Pig could not eat the yellow apple. And my big watermelon went *pop*. I will never find a special something for any of my friends."

Then she came to something by a tree.

Lily Goose walked all around the thing. "I do not think it will grow," she said. "It does not look like something to eat. It is pretty to look at, but will it keep anyone cool on a hot day? If I touch it, will it pop? I guess I will leave it right here. It is not something special for any of my friends."

Lily Goose decided to go home. She went back to the path.

Fat Brown Hen was there, pecking about in the tall grass beside the path. Fat Brown Hen was so busy that she almost bumped into Lily Goose. "What are you doing way out here?" she clucked.

"I am looking for something special for my friends," explained Lily Goose. "I have found something, but I do not know what to do with it."

She took Fat Brown Hen to the thing by the tree.

"Well, well," clucked Fat Brown Hen when she saw it. "I know what to do with it. Now you have found something special, Lily Goose — something very, very special for me."

Fat Brown Hen stepped into the thing. She sat down and settled her feathers around her. "Thank you, Lily Goose," she said. "Thank you for finding this special nest for me."

Lily Goose went back to the barnyard.

She held her head up high. She was very happy.

She had found something special for one friend, at least!